For my family. My Mum, Dad, Marie & Jamie.
And Scooby & Tiddles, of course!
You mean the universe to me.
Always xxx - L.E.A.

Bloomsbury Publishing, London, Oxford, New York, New Delhi and Sydney

First published in Great Britain in 2017 by Bloomsbury Publishing Plc
50 Bedford Square, London WC1B 3DP

www.bloomsbury.com

BLOOMSBURY is a registered trademark of Bloomsbury Publishing Plc

Text and illustrations copyright © Laura Ellen Anderson 2017

The moral right of the author-illustrator has been asserted

A CIP catalogue record for this book is available from the British Library

ISBN 978 1 4088 6839 3 (HB)
ISBN 978 1 4088 6840 9 (PB)
ISBN 978 1 4088 6838 6 (eBook)

All papers used by Bloomsbury Publishing are natural, recyclable products
made from wood grown in well managed forests. The manufacturing processes
conform to the environmental regulations of the country of origin

Printed in China by Leo Paper Products, Heshan, Guangdong

1 3 5 7 9 10 8 6 4 2

LAURA ELLEN ANDERSON

I DON'T WANT CURLY HAIR

BLOOMSBURY
LONDON OXFORD NEW YORK NEW DELHI SYDNEY

NO!

I do NOT want this BIG CURLY HAIR!

It's messy and silly
and just plain UNFAIR!

Just look at these spirals,

these squiggles,

these swirls.

Too bouncy.

Too loopy.

Oh, so many curls!

Always too knotty

and fuzzy

and frizzy.

They curl

and they coil.

It's making me dizzy!

I want my hair STRAIGHT.

I want my hair . . .

smooth.

I want it to **flow** through the air when I move.

So I use a big brush,
and brush it ALL night,

for hours

and hours,

with all of my
MIGHT!

Next morning, I'm frazzled,
my brush hand is sore,

and my hair is MORE twisty
and looped than before!

I ask all my best friends to

pull it and

stretch it,

but, OUCH!
That's enough!
It's no use –

I will do it!

I try using

BIG

books

TO WEIGH DOWN

the curls.

But, NO, it does NOTHING
to flatten these twirls.

Balloons!

What a plan -
they'll make my hair
straight . . .

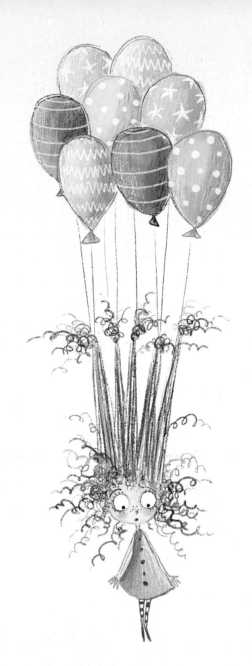

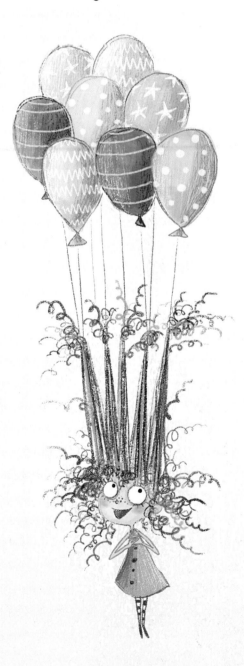

But, hang on,
what's happening?!

OH.
Now it's
too late!

I hunt down the stickiest tape I can find -
this HAS to help each of the **curls** to unwind!
But, NO, each strand **twizzles** and **wiggles** and **tangles**
and sticks out around me at mad, crazy angles!

I wet it with water, and . . . OH MY!

It's STRAIGHT!

No Curly McWurlys. It simply is GREAT!

But as my hair dries, I hear the first booOiiing
as the curls all spring up
with a ping and a dooOiiing!

It's USELESS! I give up as nothing is working —
behind every curl there's another one lurking.

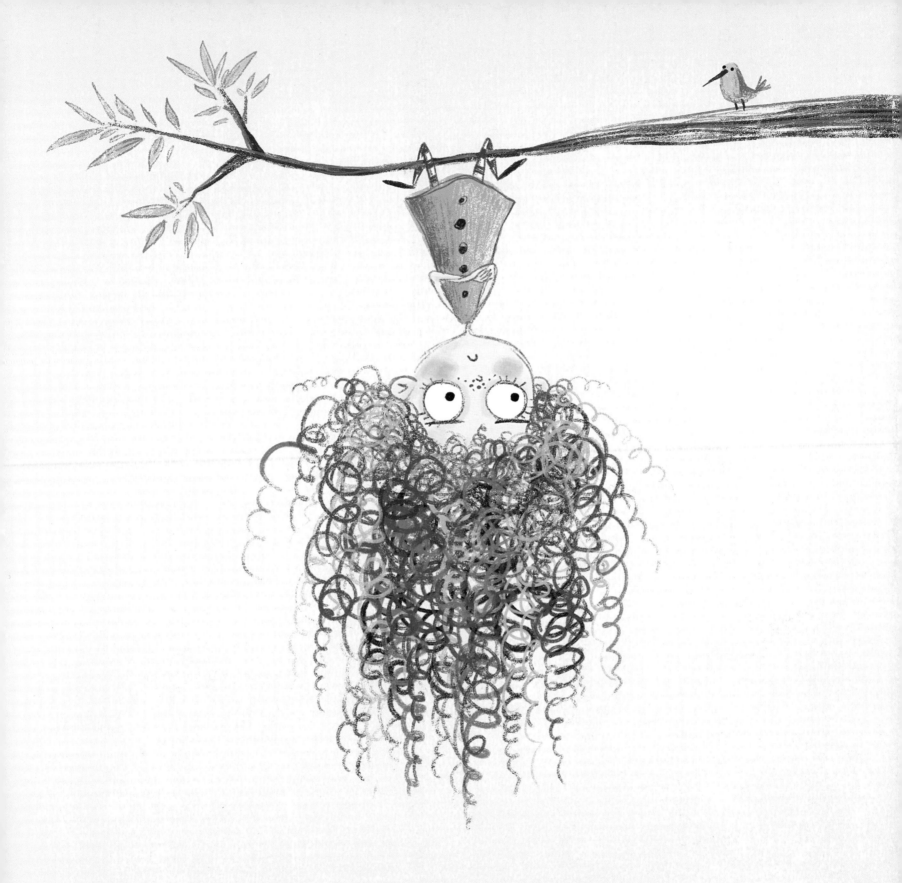

So I hang upside down in my favourite tree,
wishing my **curls** would stop bothering me.

Then, snapping me out
of my big sulky grump,
a girl STOMPS her way over
and sits in a slump.

She says, "My hair's useless!
Oh, why won't it curl?
It's boring and STRAIGHT.
There's not even ONE twirl!

I've tried **twisting**

and **spinning**

(and rolling pins, too!).

I want my hair **lovely**
and BIG just like . . .

We grin and start laughing -
how silly we've been,
with **brushing** and **sticking**
and **spins** in between!

I suddenly feel like my **curls** aren't that bad . . .
In fact, now it turns out I'm feeling quite GLAD!

We spend the whole day with our bows and our clips,
creating new styles and swapping top tips!

Pigtails

and bunches.

A beehive,

a bun!

We have hours of **fabulous** great hairy fun!

The winding, the turning, the twists everywhere –
no matter what shape or size . . .